EMPIRE DREAMS

by Wendy Wax

Illustrated by Todd Doney

SILVER MOON PRESS
NEW YORK

First Silver Moon Press Edition 2000
Copyright © 2000 by Wendy Wax
Illustrations copyright © 2000 by Todd Doney
Edited by Carmen McCain

Special thanks to Mike Phillips, retired ironworker and actor in
The Last of the Mohicans, Grady Turner of the New-York Historical Society,
and Rosemary Richmond of the American Indian Community House
for their historical direction and review.

For information:
Silver Moon Press
New York, NY
(800) 874–3320

Library of Congress Cataloging-in-Publication Data

Wax, Wendy.
    Empire dreams / by Wendy Wax ; illustrated by Todd Doney.-- 1st Silver Moon Press ed.
        p. cm. -- (Adventures in America)
    Includes bibliographical references.
    Summary: In 1930 in New York City, as she worries about the Depression's effect
on her family, eleven-year-old Julie takes a personal interest in the building of the
Empire State Building and befriends a Mohawk boy who is working on the project.
    ISBN 1-893110-19-2
    [1. Depressions--1929--Juvenile fiction. [1. Depressions--1929--Fiction. 2. New
York (N.Y.)--Fiction. 3. Empire State Building (New York, N.Y.)--Fiction. 4. Jews--
United States--Fiction. 5. Mohawk Indians--Fiction. 6. Indians of North America--
Fiction.] I. Doney, Todd, ill. II.Title. III. Series.

PZ7.W35117 Em 2000
[Fic]--dc21

                                                                    00-030770

                    10   9   8   7   6   5   4   3   2
                        Printed in the USA

To Nomi and Jon

— WW

ONE

JUNE 1930

"THE EMPIRE STATE BUILDING WILL BE 102 stories high!" eleven-year-old Julie Singer explained to her grandmother, pointing to a headline in her scrapbook. Ever since the newspapers had announced plans for the tallest skyscraper in the world, Julie had been pasting articles in a large scrapbook. It was now late June, 1930, and the construction of the Empire State Building was the biggest news since 1927 when Charles Lindbergh flew an airplane across the Atlantic Ocean.

"*Oy vay iz mir*," Grandma said, adjusting her spectacles. Grandma was always using Yiddish phrases. "Too many stairs to climb!"

"You won't have to climb, Grandma," Julie said, tossing a light brown braid over her shoulder. "There will be elevators."

"It's no use, Julie," Uncle Morris said, chuckling behind his newspaper. "You'll never convince your grandma that there's a skyscraper, brownstone—or neighborhood—better than this one."

"I like Vee-lliamsburg," Grandma insisted.

Julie giggled as Uncle Morris rolled his eyes. Until a month ago, Grandma had constantly complained about Williamsburg—their nosy neighbors, the broken front step, the unfriendly grocer, and the noisy street. But as soon as Julie's father announced that they'd be moving to Borough Park, a nicer, newer Brooklyn neighborhood, Grandma's complaining stopped. It didn't seem to matter to her that her son-in-law, an architect, had designed a house that would soon be built, or that they'd be getting a car of their own. "I haf enough change in my life already. I vant to stay here," she announced stubbornly.

Ever since Grandpa died, Grandma had been living on the ground floor of their three-story brownstone on Ross Street. The brownstone had once been nice, but every year it became more run down. There was no yard, the iron railing on the front steps was loose, and the roof leaked. The rest of the family were all for moving, so Grandma had no choice.

"Pointer!" came a cry from the open window.

Julie poked her head out and saw her older brother hit a home run.

"Go, Sammy!" she yelled as her dark haired twelve-year-old brother circled the makeshift bases. Sam was the fastest runner on the block. He had planned to work for an electrician that summer, but the day before he was to start, the electrician went out of business. Now Sam divided his time between studying for his bar mitzvah and playing stoopball, stickball, or kick the can with the other neighborhood kids.

Sam's twin, Sophie, stood nearby pitching pennies with her best friend, Betsy. Like Sam, Sophie had dark hair, but her eyes were blue-gray like Julie's. Since her twelfth birthday, Sophie had

stopped wearing braids and begun curling her long hair. "Your sister's going to be interested in boys soon," Julie's mother had said. But Julie knew it had already happened. During Betsy's turn, Julie noticed Sophie's eyes wandering over to Tony Speroni who was playing stoopball with Sam.

"Hi, Julie!" called Rachel Rabinowitz. "Wanna play?"

"No, thanks," Julie called down to the chubby girl with thick red hair. Though it was almost dinnertime, Rachel was slurping a cherry-flavored soda.

"Vhy don't you play with Rachel?" Grandma said.

"I'm tired of Rachel," Julie said, "and, anyway, it's almost dinnertime." Sometimes Julie wished she enjoyed street games like her brother and sister. But usually she preferred reading or working on her scrapbook.

"*The Brooklyn Eagle* came with a hole in it," Uncle Morris said, poking his nearly bald head through the center of a page.

"Sorry," Julie said, laughing, "but I needed that article for my scrapbook. It said that materials from all over the world are being shipped into New York to build the Empire State Building."

"Is that so?" Uncle Morris asked, eyes twinkling.

Julie nodded. "The steel came from Pittsburgh, the limestone from Indiana, and the lumber from the Pacific Coast. They even bought an entire quarry in Germany just for the marble, and . . ."

"There's not much Julie doesn't know," Mr. Singer

said from the doorway.

"Hi, Papa," Julie jumped up to give her father a hug. His graying beard tickled her face. She noticed that he looked tired, as he had all week.

"Ever since you took her to see the Waldorf-Astoria hotel being torn down, she's become an expert on the Empire State Building," Uncle Morris said. The Empire State Building was being built in place of the old hotel.

Mr. Singer nodded distractedly.

Julie remembered what a thrill it had been to watch the fancy hotel being blasted last fall. Every few minutes, dynamite exploded with a muffled thunk, causing the ground to shake and clouds of dust to rise into the air. Julie had read that several parts of the old hotel, including an elevator, would be used in the new skyscraper.

"Let's see how much you know," Uncle Morris said.

"Ask me anything," Julie said, plopping down on the sofa next to Grandma.

"Who's the president of the Empire State Building project?"

"Alfred Smith," Julie said. Alfred E. Smith was a powerful, well-liked figure. He had once been the governor of New York State and had run in the country's presidential election.

"Who's paying for it?" asked Uncle Morris, a smile tugging at the corners of his mouth.

"John Raskob and Pierre du Pont," Julie said, proudly. The two wealthy men hadn't lost all their money when the stock market crashed in the fall, allowing them to continue construction during the recent hard times.

"You sure do know your facts," Uncle Morris said.

Mrs. Singer walked into the room holding a serving spoon. She wore a blue dress and her curly, dark hair was pulled back in a bun. "Julie, will you call Sophie and Sam?" she asked. "Dinner's ready."

Julie stuck her head out the window. "Sam! Soph—"

"That's not what I meant, Julie," Mrs. Singer said. "Please go out and get them."

"Yes, Mama," Julie said, rising from the sofa.

Julie went downstairs and stood on the front stoop. Though the sun was setting, the street was still filled with activity. It would be like that all summer—old people talking on fire escapes and stoops, children playing games in the street, babies crying, dogs barking, people riding bicycles, and radios playing in the background. She wondered if she'd miss their street when they moved.

"Sammy!" Julie called to her brother who was still playing stickball. "Dinner!"

"Fins," Sam called, which meant *time out*. He waved to his friends and headed home.

"Where's Sophie?" Julie asked.

Sam shrugged. "She knows she has to be home before sundown."

Julie and Sam went upstairs and found Grandma, Uncle Morris, Aunt Esther, and Mr. Singer sitting at the neatly set dining room table.

Aunt Esther and Uncle Morris had Sabbath dinner

at the Singer's house on Friday nights. It was the only time they ate a traditional Jewish meal.

"Sammy, where's your sister?" Mrs. Singer asked, as Sam washed his hands.

Sam shrugged. "Last I saw, she was with Betsy."

Julie knew her sister would come in any minute with a long, complicated excuse. She always did.

"Well, she won't get Sabbath dinner at the Bordonaro home," Aunt Esther said. Betsy's family was Italian.

"I hope she isn't roaming around Division Street," Mrs. Singer said, frowning as she placed the fresh loaf of challah on the table. She preferred her children to stay on the south side of Division Street—not the north side where Betsy's family lived in a six-story tenement.

"Don't be too hard on her," Aunt Esther said. "Having to go to summer school is bad enough." Sophie was enrolled in summer school at Public School 16 to make up for the month she'd been out sick in the winter. Aunt Esther always stuck up for Julie and her sister and brother. She was ten years younger than Julie's mother and never took things as seriously. She had brown curly hair like her sister but was shorter and plumper.

"Maybe you're right, Esther," Mrs. Singer said, "but we're not going to wait for her."

Everyone watched Mrs. Singer light the candles and say the blessing. After saying *Amen* they helped themselves to the delicious roasted chicken, sweet potatoes, noodle pudding, peas, and challah.

"You look pretty in that shawl," Aunt Esther said to Grandma as she poured water in her glass.

"It is the von Julie embroidered for me," Grandma said, holding up the lace-embroidered edge.

"I have a very talented niece," Aunt Esther said, smiling at Julie.

"And nephew," Sam said, buttering a piece of challah. "I've hit so many home runs this week, I'll be playing in Ebbets Field with the Dodgers soon."

"But how are your sewing skills?" Uncle Morris asked.

"Not as good as Julie's," Sam said, grinning.

Julie was used to getting compliments. She, Sophie, and their mother were all good with the needle. They did their best work by hand.

"We could use you at the factory," Uncle Morris said to Julie, scooping some noodle pudding. He and Aunt Esther manufactured collars for ladies' dresses at Greenberg's Dress Collar Manufacturers, the company Grandpa had started in Manhattan. They lived in Manhattan as well.

"I like to sew, but I'd rather be an architect like Papa," Julie said.

"You are lucky you don't haf to vork," Grandma said. "Vhen I vas your age I vork tvelve hours a day making silk decorations for ladies' hats and I . . ."

". . . didn't know a word of English," Julie finished for her. She had heard Grandma's stories about leaving Russia hundreds of times.

"And vhen your mother vas a girl, she had vork too."

"But less than eight hours a day," said Mrs. Singer, passing the peas to Mr. Singer. "By then, your grandfather owned the place."

"Julie, you are very fortunate your father makes good living," said Grandma.

"I know," said Julie, looking proudly at her father. Again, she noticed how tired he looked—and worried. But these days everyone looked tired and worried. The stock market crash the previous October had caused the whole business structure of the city to collapse. Many businesses had shut down and thousands of people were now unemployed. Wages and rents had dropped, stores and offices stood empty, and crowds of people looking for jobs stood in line at employment offices. Even some of the wealthiest people in the city had been affected.

"Enough about business," Mr. Singer said, impatiently.

They heard feet pounding up the stairs. Seconds later, Sophie burst into the dining room.

"Sorry I'm late," she said, breathlessly, "but it's more Julie's fault than mine."

"My fault?" Julie exclaimed, as her sister hurried into the kitchen to wash her hands. *This better be good*, she thought.

TWO

"THERE'S NO EXCUSE FOR BEING LATE," Mr. Singer said, as Sophie joined them at the table. "You have a curfew."

"And why is it Julie's fault?" Sam asked.

"If Mikey Peterson didn't have a crush on you, Julie, he wouldn't have stopped me on my way back from Betsy's—" Sophie looked guiltily at her mother. "I just walked Betsy up to Division and turned around." She looked back at Julie. "On my way home, Mikey Peterson saw me and babbled on and on until he finally had the guts to give me this." She pulled a colorful, beaded bracelet from her pocket and handed it to her younger sister. "For you."

"I won't wear it," Julie said, though she couldn't help admiring the raised pattern of red, blue, and yellow beads on a leather band. "I don't want Mikey to get the wrong idea." Mikey Peterson was a pest, and everyone on Ross Street knew he had a crush on Julie.

"Mikey's father found it on the construction site of the Empire State Building," Sophie said, eyeing the chicken platter across the table. Aunt Esther passed it to her. "Mr. Peterson is one of the on-site carpenters."

"He is?" Julie asked, intrigued. She helped herself to a sweet potato and marveled at the fact that Sophie had, once again, gotten away with coming in late.

"*Zehrshayn*," Grandma said, admiring the bracelet.

"It could belong to one of the Indian ironworkers building the skyscraper," Mr. Singer suggested.

"Indians?" Julie stared at her father in amazement. She imagined Buffalo Bill, one of her favorite dime novel characters, tying his horse at the foot of the growing skyscraper. "Since when are Indians working on the Empire State Building?"

"Finally a fact that Julie doesn't know!" Uncle Morris said, grinning.

"Why haven't you told me about these Indians, Papa?" Julie said, ignoring her uncle.

"I don't know much about them," said Mr. Singer, pushing his plate away. Julie noticed he had barely touched his food. "All I know is that they build bridges and skyscrapers."

"I thought Indians live on reservations," Sam said.

"Many do," Mr. Singer said. "But the men often leave for months at a time to work in cities where there are a lot of buildings going up."

"And you haven't told me this?" Julie asked.

"I've heard they walk along beams way up in the sky as if they were walking on the ground," said Mr. Singer.

"That's amazing!" Julie exclaimed. She tried to imagine herself that far above ground and shivered.

"Are all the ironworkers Indians?" Sam asked, reaching for the chicken platter.

"Not all, but many of them," Mr. Singer said.

"Why haven't they been mentioned in the newspapers?" Julie asked, wiping her hands on her napkin.

"People are more interested in facts about the building than the people who are working on it," Aunt Esther said.

"Well, I'm interested in the Indians," Julie said, fastening the bracelet around her wrist.

"Mikey will be so happy," Sophie teased her sister. "I don't know what he'll do without you when we go to the Catskills."

"We're not going to the Catskills," Mr. Singer said, rubbing his face wearily. "I've been meaning to . . ." Everyone looked at Mr. Singer with surprise. For the past four or five years, the whole family had spent every August at a hotel in the mountains.

"Why not?" Julie asked. It was hard to imagine a summer without swimming in the lake, reading on the wide verandah, and falling asleep to the sound of crickets.

"Times are hard, Julie," Mr. Singer sighed. "Even for me."

"But you still haf vork," Grandma said, sounding concerned.

"You have nothing to worry about," Mr. Singer said, twisting his napkin in his hands. "But we have to start being more careful with money."

"Does that mean no car?" asked Sam.

"That's what it means," said Mr. Singer.

Julie knew her father's architecture firm hadn't been doing as well as usual, but that was to be expected with hard times.

"I guess ve von't be moving to Borough Park." said Grandma, suddenly looking cheerful.

"Not for a while," Mr. Singer said, avoiding all their eyes.

Everyone was silent. Julie wondered if the large house he had been designing for a wealthy family in Coney Island had fallen through. During times like these, it seemed a miracle that the Empire State Building continued to rise so quickly.

"Won't President Hoover fix things by August?" Julie asked with concern.

"He hasn't done much so far," Uncle Morris said with a shrug.

"It's still too early to tell," said Mrs. Singer. She watched Sam work his way through a third helping of noodle pudding.

"Don't vorry, Julie," said Grandma. "Your father is an intelligent man. Your aunt and uncle are intelligent too. That's vhy they're not going out of business like so many others."

"Mother, it's not that we're smart," protested Aunt Esther. "We're just lucky that dress collars are practical."

"Anna Katz's father's fur coat factory closed down," said Sophie.

"Who buys fur coats during times like these?" asked Sam.

"Let's talk about something besides business," Mr. Singer said with frustration.

"Can we go to Coney Island instead of the Catskills, Papa?" Sophie asked. "It only costs a nickel for the subway, and the beach is free."

"Every time we go to Coney Island, you children manage to spend a fortune," said Mrs. Singer.

"We must cut back on all luxuries," said Mr. Singer. "Do you children understand?" He looked at each one of them.

"Yes, Papa," they said together.

After dinner, Julie went into the bedroom she shared with Sophie to read her favorite Buffalo Bill adventure, while Sophie did the dishes by herself as a punishment for being late. Sam returned to the street to play stickball until dark.

"You're still wearing the bracelet," Sophie said later as the girls got ready for bed.

"I like it," Julie said, "which doesn't mean I like Mikey. I'll take it off when I see him."

* * *

The next morning, Mrs. Singer sent Julie and Sophie out to the Italian vendor's cart to buy carrots, radishes, and plum tomatoes. The day was warm and sunny, and the noisy street was crowded with pedestrians, vendors, cars, and horse carriages.

The air was filled with the mixed aroma of garlic, horse manure, body odor, and fresh bread. They waved to the milkman as he passed by in his truck. At the intersection of Lee Avenue and Roebling Street, they waited for the maroon-and-cream-colored trolley to pass before crossing. The streetcar could be operated from both ends. When the motorman reached the end of the line, he'd get out, pull down one pole, put up another, and continue back in the direction he had come. Passengers leaned out the windows, watching the people on the streets.

"Sophie! Julie!"

The two sisters turned to find Sophie's best friend, Betsy, rushing toward them. Betsy's black curls were in disarray, and her green eyes were red and puffy.

"What's the matter, Betsy?" Sophie asked.

"We're moving to New Jersey," Betsy said, trying to catch her breath. "Your mom told me which way you'd be walking. Papa's bakery has gone out of business. He thinks we'll be better off on my cousin's farm, where there'll always be food on the table."

"But you *can't* move," Sophie said, her eyes filling with tears. She threw her arms around her best friend.

"Maybe you could live with us," Julie offered.

"I have no choice," Betsy said, wiping her eyes. "We're leaving tomorrow afternoon, and I have to go home and help Mama pack."

"When can I see you then?" Sophie asked.

"This is it," Betsy said. "I'll write you a letter." She let go of Sophie and hugged Julie. "Tell your sister she has to write me back."

"I will," said Julie, knowing that Sophie didn't like to write letters. Seconds later, Betsy disappeared back down the crowded street, hurrying home to help her mother.

"Maybe Betsy's family will move back when things get better," Julie said, consolingly.

"I doubt it," Sophie said, bitterly. "I don't know what I'd do if Papa ever lost his job. Where would we move to?" Julie didn't know the answer.

They purchased the vegetables from the Italian

vendor and then headed home in silence. Julie felt terrible for her sister. "Why don't you bake Betsy a a farewell cake?" Julie suggested.

"Good idea," Sophie said, brightening a little. "I'll bake it this afternoon and bring it to her tomorrow morning before she leaves."

When they got home, Sophie started baking in the kitchen while Julie sat out on the stoop with scissors, paste, and her Empire State Building scrapbook. She had three new articles to add.

"Hi, Julie," Mikey Peterson called from the sidewalk. His blond hair was neatly combed and his freckles as plentiful as ever. "You're wearing it!"

"What?" Julie asked, as she followed his gaze to her wrist. She had forgotten to take off the bracelet. "It's not what you think, Mikey. I think it's pretty but . . ."

Mikey blushed and climbed to the top step. "It's an Indian bracelet. My father found it," he said, sitting down beside her.

"That's what my dad thought," Julie said. "Do you know where the Indians live?"

"Yeah," Mikey said. "North Gowanus."

"Really?" Julie said, looking at Mikey with a new respect. "That's pretty close!" North Gowanus was in Brooklyn, south of Williamsburg, on the opposite side of Fort Greene Park.

"Wanna see where they live?" Mikey asked. "We could go tomorrow."

"Sure," Julie said, amazed that she was actually saying *yes* to Mikey Peterson. "But don't you go to church on Sunday?"

"Good point," Mikey said, turning red. "When should we go?" He was determined not to let the opportunity slip away.

"Go where?" Sam asked, coming toward them. His shirt and pants were stained with dirt and sweat from his morning stickball game in the park.

"To North Gowanus," Mikey said, "to see where the Indians live."

"I want to come," Sam said.

"Let's go Monday," Mikey said.

"The Indians won't be there," Julie said. "They'll be at work in Manhattan."

"I guess you're right," Mikey said.

"But let's go anyway," Julie said. "At least this way, we can see where they live."

"Don't you have to be at the Y, Julie?" Sam asked his sister. Julie was spending summer weekdays at the Young Men's and Young Women's Hebrew Association. In the mornings she stuffed envelopes with other volunteers her age. In the afternoons, she participated in group athletics—but the only one she liked was swimming. The girls swam Mondays and Wednesdays, the boys swam Tuesdays and Thursdays.

"No one seems to care if I'm there or not," Julie said. "It's not like school."

"Well, okay," Sam said. "But we can't tell anyone. Mama would have a fit if she knew we went past Fort Greene Park."

The sound of their father yelling drifted out the door.

"I wonder what that's all about," Sam said, looking

up at the living room window.

They went inside and found their father sitting on the sofa, now talking calmly to Sophie who sat beside him. Mrs. Singer sat nearby, mending a pair of Sam's socks. A sweet aroma filled the air.

"What's going on?" Sam asked.

Mr. Singer gestured for Julie and Sam to sit down next to Sophie, who looked like she'd been crying. "I found your sister baking a cake for Betsy."

"What's wrong with that?" Sam asked.

"It was my idea," Julie said.

"That's what I was trying to tell Papa," Sophie said, shooting a grateful look at Julie.

"Didn't I tell you we'd have to start giving up luxuries?" Mr. Singer said, looking at each of them. "A cake is a luxury. Some families don't even have a roof over their heads, let alone sugar, flour, and butter."

"I said I'm sorry, Papa," Sophie said.

"She was just being thoughtful," said Mrs. Singer, looking up from her mending.

"I apologize for overreacting," Mr. Singer said, gently. "You can take the cake to Betsy this time. But after that, no more baking cakes. Do you understand?"

"Yes, Papa," Julie, Sam, and Sophie said together.

That night, Julie lay in bed thinking about what her father had said. She wasn't used to him yelling, and she had never really thought of cake as a luxury before. She wondered if Sophie, Sam, or her mother had noticed how strange he had been acting lately. Was it just because he was tired and worried about work? Or was there something else on his mind?

THREE

ON MONDAY MORNING, JULIE AND SOPHIE left the brownstone together, carrying their lunches in linen sacks. When they reached Lee Street, Sophie turned right in the direction of the public school, which was one block over. Julie turned left and walked over to Bedford Avenue, an elm tree-lined street with a mixture of Victorian mansions, churches, fancy clubhouses, brownstones, and apartment buildings. Instead of going south toward the YM-YWHA, she waited for Sam and Mikey on the corner.

"Hi, Julie," Mikey said, eyeing the beaded bracelet. "You look nice today." Sam winked at his sister.

I should give the bracelet back, Julie thought as she thanked Mikey for his compliment. But she liked it too much. She wondered if she really looked nice in her navy blue sailor dress or if it was just Mikey who thought so. *He'd probably think I looked nice if I was covered with mud and had no teeth*, she thought.

"Let's go to Lee Street and take the trolley to Fort Greene Park," Sam said. "Then we can walk to Atlantic Avenue and find a trolley that goes to North Gowanus."

"You really have this all figured out, Sam," Julie said, impressed. They started walking.

"I did too," Mikey said, "but Sam beat me to it."

Just as they reached Lee Street, the trolley arrived. They raced toward it, climbed aboard, and dropped their nickels in the fare box.

"I get the jump seat!" Sam said, climbing into the wooden seat behind the motorman.

"Sam, let's let Julie sit there," Mikey suggested in a grown-up voice.

"All right," Sam said, reluctantly. He followed Mikey toward the back while Julie sat down. She liked sitting in the jump seat, and it was rare to find it empty. *Mikey really isn't that bad*, she thought. *I'm just not interested in him that way.*

She gazed out the window as they passed department stores, barber shops, delicatessens, dance halls, poolrooms, and markets. The streets were crowded with trolleys, produce vendors, barking dogs, and gasoline-powered cars and buses, which were becoming more and more popular. She could see the tower of the more than twenty-six story Williamsburgh Savings Bank, the tallest building in Brooklyn. It wasn't nearly as tall as the Chrysler Building in Manhattan, and soon the Empire State Building would be even taller than that.

"That's a pretty bracelet."

Julie turned to see a dark-haired lady with nice eyes and a warm smile.

"Thank you." Julie shouted to be heard above the racket. "I think an Indian made it."

"You're probably right," said the lady. "I'm an Indian myself. Mohawk-Iroquois tribe, and I'd recognize our craftwork anywhere."

Julie moved closer to the lady so she could hear her better.

"Do you live in North Gowanus?" Julie asked with interest.

"No," the lady said, "but I know several men who do. Most of them are ironworkers. My father's cousin used to live there. He helped build Hell Gate Bridge—that's the one that connects Queens and Ward's Island—and . . ." She drifted off in thought.

"And what?" Julie asked, impatiently.

"He stepped off a scaffold into the river, and drowned," the lady said, sadly.

Julie looked with horror at the lady who remained calm. "He was the famous Joe Diabo, or Indian Jack," she said, proudly. "If the job's challenging, our men are there. Some people call them Skywalkers."

"Skywalkers," Julie said. "The sound of it makes me dizzy. Aren't they afraid of falling?" Before she could hear the lady's answer, Mikey grabbed her and led her toward the door.

"We have to switch trolleys," he said. The next trolley came ten minutes later, and soon they were stepping down onto the sidewalk surrounding Fort Greene Park.

A black iron fence with openings at each end surrounded the park. Sunlight trickled through the leaves onto the rich, green grass.

"What in the world are all these men doing here?" Sam asked, gazing through the gate.

"Why aren't they at work?" Mikey asked.

Julie looked around the park, astonished to see

that the benches were filled with men wearing suits, ties, and Fedoras. Some had briefcases, and most read newspapers. The sight was so odd—especially for a Monday morning—that Julie didn't even notice the latest *Daily News* headline read: EMPIRE STATE BUILDING: EIGHTH WONDER OF THE WORLD.

"Who are all these men?" she whispered. "And what are they doing in the park?"

Sam looked puzzled too. "They're certainly not doing business."

"And it's too early for them to be on their lunch break," said Mikey.

"They must be out of work," Julie said, feeling a wave of sadness. In their well-made suits and Fedora hats, the men didn't look like street beggars. They looked like they could be friends of her father, or the fathers of her school friends.

"I wonder why they're in the park," said Sam. "They look like they have nice homes and families. I would think they'd rather stay home where it's comfortable."

"Maybe they're hiding out in the park because they're too embarrassed to tell their families," Julie said.

"You may be right," Mikey said. "My uncle had a hard time telling my cousins that he had to close two of his hardware stores. They've been in our family for forty years!"

"They can't all be keeping secrets from their families," said Sam, as they started walking through the park. "I bet they don't like staying home because

it reminds them that they have families to care for."

"If I ever found out Papa was out of work, I'd get a job," said Julie.

"He would never let you do that," said Sam. "And it would never happen anyway. Papa's a successful architect."

"Betsy's father was a successful baker," said Julie. "You never know what's going to happen."

"Julie!" Sam stopped walking and pointed toward a bench beside a magnolia tree. "Doesn't that man look familiar?"

Julie recognized the gray-haired man with spectacles who was holding the newspaper close to his eyes. "That's Mr. Plotnick," she said, recognizing their near-sighted butcher. "The butcher. Mama went to his shop last week and thought it odd that the store was closed in the middle of the day."

"Now we know why," said Mikey.

"This is really strange," said Sam. "Let's get out of here."

Julie started to follow the boys. Seeing all the men out of work made her feel sad. *What a waste*, she thought. Most of the men seemed to be healthy and capable of hard work. Whenever one of them looked up, she smiled at him. Not that it would help their troubles, but she hoped it would help their moods.

Suddenly, Julie froze. There, on a bench less than ten feet away was her father! Julie gasped. Her first instinct was to call "Papa!" but something made her hold back. Something told her that her father didn't want to be seen.

FOUR

CONFUSED, JULIE DASHED BEHIND A TREE so she could get a better look without being caught. What was Papa doing there? Was he on his lunch break? But it wasn't even 11:00 yet and there was too much distance between the park and his office on Marcy Avenue in Williamsburg. Julie's heart sank as she realized the probable truth of the matter. Could her father's business have failed? Was he afraid to tell his family?

She wanted to run up to him and tell him that everything would be okay, but would it? How could everything be okay if her father was out of work? Even if Uncle Morris helped out, he couldn't support a family of five during these hard times! Julie remembered the conversation Friday night at the dinner table. *No wonder we're not going to the Catskills this summer,* she realized. *No wonder we might not move to Borough Park and get a car. No wonder he got so mad about the cake. I must tell Sam and Sophie,* she thought. But why get her brother and sister upset? If her father wanted them to know, wouldn't he have told them? Something told her that her mother didn't know either. Otherwise he wouldn't have said he was going to work.

Julie felt guilty for spying. She looked around for Mikey and Sam, but they had disappeared in the crowd. Just then, Mr. Singer looked away from the paper. Julie felt her heart thumping in her chest. Had he seen her? What could she say to him?

As she watched, he reached into his pocket and pulled out a pocket knife. He carefully cut out an article in the newspaper. Maybe he had found something in the "Help Wanted" section.

Julie waited until her father started reading the paper again before making her escape. She hurried in the direction Mikey and Sam had gone and was relieved to find them under a tree.

"There she is!" cried Mikey.

"What's wrong, Julie?" Sam asked. "You look like you've seen a ghost."

"I'm all right," Julie said, trying her best to sound calm. "I was just a little nervous when I thought I'd lost you."

"Well, let's head to North Gowanus," Sam said.

"I don't feel like going anymore," Julie said.

"Are you sure you're okay?" Sam asked. Julie nodded. "Well, just don't tell Mama that I went. Come on, Mikey."

"I . . . uh . . . I don't want to go anymore either," Mikey said. "Let's go home. We can play stickball."

"I can't go home," Julie said. "I'm supposed to be at the Y." She suddenly wished she hadn't missed swimming.

"Then we'll go to the park," Sam said. The park was two blocks away from the Singer's brownstone on Ross Street. "I don't feel like going all the way to North Gowanus alone."

Julie hoped that park wasn't filled with unemployed men too.

*   *   *

That evening, Julie and Sophie set the table while their mother prepared dinner. When Julie heard Mr. Singer come in, her heart skipped a beat.

"Something smells good," he called, entering the kitchen. "Hello, girls."

"Hi, Papa," Sophie said, hugging him.

"Don't I get a hug, Julie?" Mr. Singer said.

"Of course," Julie said, unable to look him in the eye. She could tell he was straining to sound happy, covering up what he really must be feeling. She wished he would stop pretending and be honest with her and the rest of the family.

"Aren't you forgetting something?" Mr. Singer said. Julie looked confused.

"The newspapers," said Mr. Singer. "Every time I come home, you ask me for the newspapers."

"Oh," Julie said, distractedly. "Do you have the newspapers?"

"As a matter of fact, I cut two articles out for you," said Mr. Singer. He reached into his pocket and handed Julie a clipping. "It's about the builders," he said. "I thought you'd be interested." Julie realized she had watched him clip it out of the newspaper. He hadn't been looking in the "Help Wanted" section after all.

Though her mind—for a change—wasn't on the

Empire State Building, Julie pretended to be interested and tried to focus on the article.

Actually, the article was interesting. It said that about 3,000 men worked on the building every day—from carpenters and bricklayers to plumbers and electricians.

"Why doesn't it mention that a lot of these iron-workers are Indians?" Julie asked.

"Your guess is as good as mine," Mr. Singer said, shrugging.

Sam grabbed the second article. "It says here that they're finishing almost one story per day!" he said incredulously. He handed the article to Julie.

"Thanks, Papa," Julie said, avoiding her father's eyes.

That evening as they got ready for bed, Julie considered telling her sister about seeing their father in Fort Greene Park. "What do you think would happen if Papa lost his business?" she asked, deciding to feel it out first.

"I don't think that would happen," Sophie said, looking at Julie through the mirror.

"It might," Julie said, seriously. "If it does, I'm going to get a real job."

"Mama and Papa wouldn't let you," Sophie said. "Neither would Grandma. And anyway I'm sure she'd help us out with money."

"You mean Uncle Morris would help us out," said Julie. "That's where Grandma gets her money—from the business."

"Whatever," said Sophie. "I just know that none of

them would want us to do anything other than charity work. We have more money than most people."

Julie decided not to share her secret with Sophie. She was already upset enough about Betsy's leaving. And it wouldn't be right to betray their father. If he wanted to keep it a secret, it wasn't up to her to let it out.

That night, Julie tossed and turned, unable to fall asleep. She was angry at her father for keeping such an important thing from his family, but she also felt sorry for him. *We all count on Papa to be strong*, she thought. She couldn't imagine what it must be like to carry that much responsibility. She just wanted to hear from her father that everything would be all right. But she had a sick feeling that he wouldn't be able to assure them of that at all.

She tried desperately to think of something she could say to him that wouldn't hurt his pride. She wished there were some way she could help.

Suddenly she remembered what Uncle Morris had said at Sabbath dinner: *"We could use you at the factory."* Despite the fact that he'd been joking, he and Aunt Esther had been very impressed by the shawl she'd embroidered for Grandma. Maybe she could persuade them to let her work part time at the factory. Though she'd had dreams of working alongside her father, who knew what the future would bring? For now, sewing would have to do. At least she was good at it. Her mother and grandmother worked when they were her age so why shouldn't she?

Suddenly her mind was racing with plans. She

knew how to get to her aunt and uncle's factory. She'd take the train to Pennsylvania Station in Manhattan the next day. She had never gone to Manhattan alone—her parents wouldn't allow it. But this was a special case. She decided against telling Sophie and Sam, who weren't very good at keeping secrets. If her parents ever found out, she'd be punished for years. But hadn't her father taught her to do what she felt was right? Well, nothing else felt as right as this.

I'm going to get a job! she thought, feeling a shiver down her spine. Then she drifted off to sleep.

FIVE

THE NEXT MORNING, JULIE WALKED Sophie to the end of the street. But as soon as Sophie headed toward school, Julie turned around and started toward the elevated station.

The station was crowded with people waiting for the steel subway car that would take them across the Williamsburg Bridge into Manhattan. As Julie paid ten cents for a round-trip fare, she noticed that her hands were trembling. She had never felt so many things at once—excitement, fear, and determination being only a few. She had been to Manhattan many times before, but never alone. As she waited for the elevated BMT line, she clutched tightly to her lunch sack and purse, watching other people on the platform. Most of them were men in suits and bowler hats and looked like they had a purpose. Julie wished her father had business to take care of, too.

She stepped back as the platform began to vibrate. Seconds later, the train sped along the tracks to a screeching stop. Julie got on with everyone else. *So far, so good*, she thought with relief. She fit in perfectly with the other passengers—an anonymous person with business to attend to in the city. She felt so grown up! Her older brother and sister had never done anything so daring. *As long as I'm back for supper, no one will ever know*, she told herself.

She switched trains at Canal Street and soon arrived at Pennsylvania Station. "Penn Station!" the conductor cried out as the train slowed to a halt. The doors opened and people hurried out of the crowded train, pushing their way toward the stairways.

When she reached the sidewalk, the first thing Julie noticed was that many of the people around her were looking up above the bustling street toward the east. She followed their gaze, squinting toward the sun, and caught her breath. There—rising up toward the sky, higher than any other building—was the Empire State Building's stainless steel mooring mast. Julie's father had given her a copy of an architectural magazine that said Mr. Lamb, the architect, had modeled the building after a sharpened pencil. She had read that at 102 stories high, it would be about a quarter of a mile above Fifth Avenue. It was to be a mooring place for dirigibles with a built-in landing platform for passengers who had flown across the Atlantic Ocean. Aside from it being the tallest skyscraper in the world, the Empire State Building would be the first one equipped for a future age of transportation.

Though she was eager to get to her aunt and uncle's factory, she couldn't resist walking the two long blocks to the construction site. *I'll only go for a few minutes*, she promised herself.

As she walked toward Fifth Avenue, she kept her eyes on the steel skeleton in the sky. She watched with awe as workers, seemingly no larger than ants, walked along the steel beams below the mooring

mast. *They must be the Skywalkers*, she thought. And they seemed to be doing just that. According to the newspapers, it was going up at a record-breaking four-and-a-half stories a week! As of last week, twenty-six stories had been completed.

She continued looking up—until she stumbled over the leg of a small, whimpering boy. He was sitting on the ground next to his mother and sister who were begging for food. Julie felt a lump in her throat. There seemed to be more poor people in the streets of Manhattan than in Brooklyn. She had heard that there were long breadlines in every major city in the United States. These people were lucky to get a piece of bread and a bowl of soup. "Share this with your family," she said, handing her lunch to the boy. She knew she'd be hungry later, but at least she knew there would be dinner on the table.

The sidewalk was crowded with people marveling at the towering skyscraper. The closer Julie got, the harder it was to see the construction; crowds and buildings obstructed her view. She made her way underneath carefully constructed bridge bungalows, which she had read housed the general contractor's offices. Next to the offices was a special entrance just for ambulances.

The crowd was so dense it took Julie fifteen minutes just to get from Sixth Avenue to Fifth. *They must all be unemployed*, Julie thought. *Otherwise, they'd be at work.* Reading about the crowds in the news had not prepared her for being among them. She had read that people watched from as far back as

Macy's on Sixth Avenue, where bleachers had been set up. At least it was an exciting way to spend a day.

Finally at Fifth Avenue, Julie squirmed her way to the front of the crowd toward a boarded fence surrounding the site. She spotted a hole in the fence and crouched down to see through it.

There were just as many people on the other side of the fence as there were on the street, though the men on the inside were wearing work clothes and moving purposefully—entering or leaving through one of the doors on the main floor of the building.

Of all the construction sites her father had taken her to see, this one was the neatest and most orderly. The builders, Starrett Brothers & Eken, Incorporated, kept all the materials inside on the basement and main floors rather than littering the grounds outside.

"I wish I were young and strong again," said a man with an English accent. He peered through a hole next to Julie. "I used to be a rigger in my younger days."

"What's a rigger?" Julie asked.

"See those two men unloading that truck?" the man asked. Julie nodded. "They're riggers. Riggers unload, move, and install heavy operating equipment such as furnaces and boilers."

Julie would have liked to talk to the man longer, but she suddenly remembered that she was in the city to find work. Though it was hard to pull herself away, she knew she had no choice.

Julie walked down Fifth Avenue. Almost everyone else was walking toward her, not just to see the

Empire State Building but to shop as well. B. Altman's department store was across the street from the skyscraper site and Tiffany's was three blocks north. Few people these days could afford to shop for clothing and jewelry, but anyone could window-shop.

At Twenty-ninth Street, she made a right and headed toward Seventh Avenue. As she walked toward her aunt and uncle's factory, she began to feel nervous. Maybe this hadn't been such a good idea. After all, she'd thought it up while half asleep.

Too late now, Julie thought, as she neared the brick, four-story building with GREENBERG'S DRESS COLLAR MANUFACTURERS stenciled in bold white lettering. Inside, the stairwell was hot and stuffy. When she reached the third floor, she found the door open and wandered into a large, high-ceilinged loft crowded with piles of material, hanging dresses, scraps of lace, scissors, rulers, and sewing machines. Seamstresses and embroiderers sat at three long tables in the center of the room. She recognized Nettie, a middle-aged woman, who'd been working there long before Julie was born. But Nettie and the other embroiderers were so engrossed in their work that they didn't notice her. Her uncle paid them by the piece, which meant they tried to finish as many collars as they could before sundown. Today Julie noticed six empty chairs and remembered that her aunt and uncle had let a few people go. The hard times were affecting everybody!

"Julie Mae Singer! What in the world are you doing here?"

SIX

STARTLED, JULIE FROZE AS AUNT ESTHER peered at her between two hanging dresses.

"Are you with your mother?" Aunt Esther asked, looking around.

"No," Julie said nervously.

"Are you with your father?" Julie shook her head, unable to speak. "You came to the city alone?" Aunt Esther sounded concerned.

"I . . . I . . . " Julie's heart was racing. "Please, please, please don't tell Mama or Papa."

"I wouldn't know what to tell them," said Aunt Esther. "Follow me. You look like you could use a glass of lemonade."

Grateful for a few seconds to think, Julie followed her aunt to the office in back. She wished she had planned ahead of time what she would say. She didn't want to tell her aunt and uncle about seeing her father in the park. That wouldn't be fair to him. He probably didn't want them to know either.

"Look who I found roaming among the piles," Aunt Esther said to Uncle Morris. He was at his desk going over merchandise orders.

"What brings you to the city, Julie?" he said with surprise.

"I'm looking for a job," Julie blurted out.

"A job?" Aunt Esther and Uncle Morris said together, looking surprised.

"I want to earn some money," said Julie. "I could use it for things like ice cream or paying for myself when we go to Coney Island. You know—things like that. Papa shouldn't have to pay for everything!"

"Aren't you thoughtful, Julie," Aunt Esther said, warmly, handing her a glass of lemonade. "But your father makes enough money." Then, she frowned, "He did cancel your trip to the Catskills, though."

"I'm sure David is doing fine," Uncle Morris said confidently. "Otherwise he would have said something to us. After all, we're family."

Their reassuring words relieved Julie. Maybe her aunt and uncle were right. Maybe her father was planning to ask for help. But then she remembered seeing him in the park. He hadn't looked like he wanted anyone to know his secret.

"I know Papa's doing fine," Julie lied. "But what if we have an emergency? What if President Hoover doesn't do anything to stop these hard times?"

"Where are you getting these ideas?" Uncle Morris asked.

"From you." Julie felt a lump in her throat and looked down at the floor, hoping she wouldn't cry. "You said you could use me at the factory."

Uncle Morris looked confused.

"Actually, she's right, Morris," Aunt Esther said. "You said it Friday night at dinner when we were admiring the shawl she made for my mother."

"So I did," Uncle Morris said, looking from Julie to his wife. "I don't like to go back on my word, Esther. Is there any piecework we can give her?"

Julie looked hopefully at her aunt. *Please, please, please,* she thought to herself.

"Julie," Aunt Esther said softly. "I'd like to help you, but I can't go behind my sister's back like that. We both know your mother would be furious if she knew you were here today asking for a job."

"I know Mama wouldn't understand," Julie said, trying a different tactic. "But I thought you would. You usually understand me."

Aunt Esther glanced at Uncle Morris and sighed. "I'll give you some piecework, Julie, because you're very determined and we're a bit short-staffed. But you'll have to find a place to do it."

"Why can't I do it here?" Julie asked, gesturing toward Nettie and the other workers.

"I wouldn't feel comfortable knowing you're here working for me while your mother thinks you're doing charity work," Aunt Esther said. "And if your mother were to stop by . . ."

"I'll work at home in my room," Julie interrupted.

"Then your mother would find out," said Aunt Esther. "Maybe this isn't such a good . . ."

"It's a great idea!" Julie said, hurriedly. "I hardly know anyone at the Y yet, so no one will miss me. And, anyway, I know a place where I can work."

"Where?" her aunt and uncle asked together.

"If I keep it a secret, you'll have nothing to hide," Julie said. "The place is safe and comfortable."

"A friend's house?" Uncle Morris asked with raised eyebrows.

Julie nodded, unable to voice the lie. If her aunt and uncle knew she had no idea where she was going to work, they might not give it to her.

"Very well," said Aunt Esther. "I'll pay you by the piece. How does fifteen cents a piece sound?"

"Perfect!" Julie said.

Her aunt brought her three collars that needed identical embroidered flower patterns. "Start with these," she said. "They'll fit easily into your bag."

"Thank you, thank you, thank you!" Julie said, hugging Aunt Esther and Uncle Morris.

"I'd like you to spend an hour or so watching what our other embroiderers are doing," said Uncle Morris. "But first, how would you like some lunch?"

"I'd love some," Julie said, remembering that she had given hers away.

The three of them bought knishes from a street vendor and brought them back to the office to eat. After lunch, Nettie showed Julie everything she needed to know about embroidering a collar. Julie was surprised at how easy it looked. Not all the employees were as nice to her as Nettie, though. One gray-haired woman with squinty eyes asked her to move away because she was blocking the light.

Before Julie left, she asked her uncle why the woman had seemed angry at her.

"That's Lucy," Uncle Morris said. "I think she and some of the others are afraid that with a young, talented girl like you working for us we might not need them anymore. And some of them are supporting families."

Julie felt a wave of sadness. She had no intention of taking jobs away from anyone.

"Don't forget," Aunt Esther said as Julie prepared to leave. "Not a word to your mother."

"I promise if you promise," Julie said.

"We'll give you till Thursday afternoon," said Uncle Morris. "If you need longer, let us know."

"Will there be more work then?" Julie asked.

"Let's take one step at a time," said Aunt Esther.

Julie planned to do her best work so her aunt and uncle wouldn't be able to resist giving her more work.

Julie headed toward Penn Station. Before entering the station, she took one last look at the growing skyscraper. *The ironworkers must have gone home*, she thought.

The subway platform was crowded. When the train came, Julie squeezed her way into the car and felt lucky to find a seat. At Herald Square, Julie noticed a group of tall, dark men with shoulder length hair board the train. Most of them had high cheekbones and dark eyes. They wore work clothes and boots, and carried tools in their pockets. Although they were speaking English, the words they used were unfamiliar to Julie—all about rivets and welding and trusses and derricks and girders.

A boy about her age stood among the men. His eyes were dark and exhausted.

"It's okay, punk," one of the older men said to him. "You'll get the hang of it."

"Hey, lazy, how ya' doin'?" a man from the other

end of the group called to the boy. The boy shrugged.

"He's not used to all this action," another man said, laughing.

Soon all the men were teasing the boy. "Stop taking things so seriously, son," said a man with a gruff voice.

Julie had heard that plenty of times. Her teachers, parents, and sister were always telling her she took things too seriously. But it was hard not to!

"Don't let them push you around," the man continued. "Show them you're a real man." Julie was impressed when the boy managed a tired grin.

"I'll be all right," the boy said.

"You'd better get to sleep early, punk," one of the men said. "We have to be back at the job by sunrise tomorrow."

Julie wondered what the boy could have done to cause all the teasing. And where did they have to be at sunrise?

When the train stopped at Canal Street, Julie stood up and waited for the doors to open.

"Is this North Gowanus?" the boy said, rubbing his tired eyes.

"Not yet," said one of the men.

Suddenly Julie understood. These were the Indians! They had to be at the Empire State Building by sunrise! Now they were heading to North Gowanus.

Julie switched trains. As the train sped over the Williamsburg Bridge, she wondered if she had seen any of the men from the train walking in the sky.

SEVEN

A S JULIE CLIMBED THE STAIRS, SHE WON-
dered if anyone would notice something different
about her. Did she seem more sophisticated after
spending a day in the city on her own? She hoped no
one she knew had seen her getting on or off the
elevated on Broadway and Marcy Avenue. When she
reached the landing, she checked her watch. It was
5:15, the time she got home every day. *No one will
notice a thing*, she told herself.

She found her mother in the kitchen making dinner. Her father wasn't home yet, and Sophie was
working on her schoolwork.

Julie was bursting with the desire to tell some-
body about her day but knew it had to remain a
secret—at least for now.

When Mr. Singer came home, Julie felt the thrill
she'd been feeling all day quickly dissolve. Behind
his tired smile her father looked depressed. *Don't
feel you have to smile for us*, Julie wanted to say.

Mr. Singer handed Julie two articles about the
Empire State Building, one from the *Sun* and one from
The New York Times. Both articles were on the incred-
ible strength of the skyscraper's steel frame. It had to
be strong to carry the weight of the building and its
occupants, and to resist the sideways push of the wind.

"I thought you might have discovered these on your own," Mr. Singer said.

"No, I hadn't noticed them," said Julie, realizing it was the first day she hadn't noticed a single headline. Being at the construction site was much more exciting than reading a newspaper. She still couldn't look her father in the eye. He had always been honest with her—hadn't he? How could their relationship ever be the same now that she knew his secret?

At dinner, Sam told everyone that T. J. Berg's father disappeared after losing his money in the stock market. T. J., his sister, and their mother had to move in with neighbors until they found a better solution.

"*Oy gevalt!*" said Grandma, shaking her head.

Everyone except Julie and her father began to talk. Julie felt lonely. She had lots of news and no one to share it with. She had gone to Manhattan alone; she had seen the Empire State Building; she had gotten real piecework, and she had seen the Skywalkers!

"How was your day, Julie?" Sophie asked.

"My day?" Julie said, surprised that Sophie had thought to ask. "Same as usual." She helped herself to more potatoes.

"Then where were you at lunch?" Sophie asked.

"At lunch?" Julie asked, suddenly lightheaded.

"Mikey Peterson said he went to the Y hoping to find you," Sophie said. "He looked for you in the cafeteria and you weren't there."

"I wish he would leave me alone," Julie said, annoyed. "I wasn't hungry so I went to the library."

"Isn't the library a little far from the Y?" Sam asked innocently.

"I took a long lunch hour," Julie said, wishing everyone would stop asking her questions.

"But you have to eat," said Mrs. Singer. "And you should be with other children." She passed the carrots to Julie.

"I had a snack late in the afternoon," Julie said, remembering her lunch at her uncle's factory. At least that much was truthful.

"Speaking of the library," Sophie said, "I heard that if times keep getting worse, the Brooklyn Public Library might have to shorten their hours. They won't be able to afford paying full wages to their staff."

"That's not fair," said Julie. She went to the library frequently.

"I'll tell Mikey to look for you in the library tomorrow at lunch," Sam grinned.

"No!" Julie blushed as everyone stared at her. "I mean, I took out two books today, so I won't be going back this week."

"So you'll be in the cafeteria?" Sophie asked.

"I might be," Julie said, wishing someone would change the subject. "But I like to eat alone so I can read."

"I'd much rather eat lunch with friends," Sophie said. "Wouldn't you, Sam?" Her twin nodded with his mouth full.

"There's nothing wrong with wanting to be alone," said Mr. Singer.

Julie smiled at her father gratefully. He always

stuck up for her. She wished she had never seen him in Fort Greene Park. She wanted him to know she'd love him with or without a job. But what if he did reveal his secret? What if he said something she didn't want to hear? Her thoughts only made her more determined to make money . . . which reminded her. Where could she do the piecework? That night, she fell asleep early, without having a solution.

The next morning, after leaving Sophie at the corner of Lee Street, Julie wandered around looking for a quiet, comfortable place to work. She ruled out the parks in the neighborhood. Someone she knew might see her there—maybe even her own father. She ruled out the Brooklyn Public Library for the same reason. After an hour, she decided there was too much risk of being recognized in Williamsburg. *I guess I'll go back to Manhattan*, she thought with excitement, heading toward the elevated station.

Julie found a discarded newspaper and read it as the train cruised to Manhattan. She tore out an article about an "industrial railroad" built on every concrete floor of the Empire State Building to help move materials from one side of the floor to the other. Folding the article, she slid it into her purse.

As soon as she arrived in the city, Julie couldn't resist walking by the building again. It was like a magnet. *Maybe I'll think of a place to do my piecework while I walk*, she rationalized.

After watching for fifteen minutes, she asked a woman with a baby carriage if there was a park nearby. "Bryant Park," the woman said.

"That's the park behind the New York Public Library!" Julie said, wondering why she hadn't thought of it herself. Her father had taken her there the year before to show her where her grandparents had educated themselves when they first arrived in New York. It had two stone lions out front.

Julie made her way through the crowds on Fifth Avenue and turned west on Fortieth Street. When she reached Bryant Park, she found a familiar scene of men in dark suits and bowler hats, sitting on the benches reading newspapers. Though she'd rather have gone somewhere else, she knew she had to get the work done. She found a vacant bench on the north side of the park and sat down. Before taking the materials out of her bag, Julie squinted up in the sunlight, mesmerized by the tiny workers she saw on what she guessed was the twenty-seventh or twenty-eighth floor. They looked like spiders spinning a web. *If I keep looking up, I'll never get anything done*, Julie scolded herself. She pulled the collars, thread, and needles out of her bag and began to work.

The work was easy. Julie enjoyed the feel of the warm sun. It didn't even bother her that she had missed another swimming day. She loved the familiar feeling of the needle and thread. Even the shawl she had made for her grandmother had more complicated stitches.

Before she knew it, two hours had passed, and she had finished the first collar. Satisfied with the way it came out, she started on the second one. If she continued working at this speed, she'd be able to return them to her aunt and uncle that day—one day early!

As Julie began embroidering the second collar, she felt someone sit down at the opposite end of the bench. She turned and saw a boy about her own age staring at her hands. He had high cheekbones, smooth skin, and coal black hair. He wore dirty work clothes and boots. But what Julie noticed most were his sad, dark eyes. He didn't look very happy.

"Hello," she said. The boy didn't answer. *What could be wrong?* Julie wondered as she returned to her piecework.

Seconds later, she felt the boy staring at her again. When she looked up, he quickly moved his gaze to his hands. This happened over and over until Julie couldn't take it anymore. "Hi, I'm Julie Singer," she said.

The boy nodded. "Where did you get that bracelet?" he asked without changing his expression.

"Someone gave it to me," Julie said. "A boy . . . I mean, he's not my boyfriend or anything but . . ." She blushed. "What's your name?"

The boy cleared his throat, "Daniel A. Hill."

"What does the A stand for?" Julie asked. She had trouble understanding Daniel's answer. "A-da-ho-ra?" she asked, trying to pronounce what she had heard.

"Close enough," Daniel said, turning toward her. "It's a Mohawk name. Our alphabet only has sixteen letters and some of them are very different from English ones."

"You're an Indian?" Julie asked, feeling a wave of excitement.

Daniel nodded. "My sister makes bracelets like that," he said. "It's a Mohawk design."

"That's what I've been told," Julie said, "But—wait—isn't Daniel an English name?"

"It is," Daniel said, "so people like you can pronounce it. But my middle initial stands for my Mohawk name. That's the way it is with most of us."

"Are any of your relatives working on the Empire State Building?" Julie asked.

"Lots of them," Daniel said proudly, pointing to the towering steel structure. "See the guy in the middle?" Julie nodded. "I think that's my brother Douglas. He's only fourteen—the youngest in the gang—but he's the best."

"How can you tell it's him?" Julie asked.

"By where he's standing in relation to those two other men," Daniel said. "He's building the steel skeleton of the skyscraper, and that's about where he should be."

"There's something I've been wondering," Julie said. "If the Empire State Building is made out of steel, why are they called ironworkers?"

"Bridges and skyscrapers used to be built out of iron so I guess the name just stuck," Daniel said, pushing his dark hair out of his face.

"What about you?" Julie asked. "Do you want to be a Skywalker?"

"It doesn't matter what I want," Daniel said. "I have no choice."

EIGHT

"THEN WHY ARE YOU HERE AND NOT AT the construction site?" Julie asked looking up again. She noticed that the sky was becoming cloudy.

"They told me to get lost," Daniel said.

"What did you do that was so bad?" Julie asked.

"I spilled two quarts of water," Daniel said. "Then I brought the wrong-sized rivets."

"The wrong-sized what's-its?" Julie asked.

"Rivets," Daniel said. "I'm not old enough to be a Skywalker. My job is to do basic grunt work—deliver messages, bring ironworkers water and coffee, find the right sized rivets . . ." He pulled a small piece of steel from his pocket. "This is a rivet," he said, tossing it to Julie. She caught it.

"Good catch," Daniel said. "That's how we toss them."

"What do you mean?" Julie asked, curiously.

Daniel began to explain. "Raising gangs hoist up steel columns, beams, and girders, set them in position, and bolt them together. Fitting-up gangs tighten the pieces together. Then the four-man riveting gang makes everything permanent by using rivets instead of temporary bolts. The 'heater' stands over a pit of flaming coal all day, cooking rivets until they're red-hot. Then he tosses it with tongs about sixty feet in the air to the 'catcher' who snares it with his metal mitt."

"It sounds like baseball," Julie said.

"It's noisier than baseball." Daniel smiled. "The catcher tosses the rivet to the 'bucker-up' who uses a long tool to hold the rivet in a hole, while the 'riveter' moves in from the other side. The riveter rattles his gun against the rivet's front end until it is flattened against the hole. Rivets come in all different sizes."

"So, you mixed up rivets and spilled water." Julie said. "Everyone makes mistakes."

"Ironworkers can't afford to make mistakes," Daniel said seriously. "Whether they're walking on the highest beam or bringing water to a steel erector, they have to do it perfectly."

"Do you walk on the high beams?" Julie asked.

"Not yet," Daniel said. "But I will."

"Aren't you scared?" Julie asked. "If I were that high up, I'd be scared I'd fall."

"It's in my blood." Daniel shrugged. "My father, uncles, and all my male cousins are ironworkers. So were my grandfathers. If any of them had fears, they conquered them. I must do the same."

"But surely there are other things you can do."

"I'm proud of my heritage and in order to prove my manhood I have to become an ironworker," Daniel explained, unenthusiastically. "Otherwise, I might as well stay at the reservation with the women and girls. That's what my boss told me today. He called me a 'slowpoke'."

"Why?" Julie asked. "That's so mean."

"Well, after I spilled the water, I took the elevator

down to the floor with the food and drink vendors to get more. But by the time I returned, another boy had already beat me to it."

Julie shook her head. "That reminds me of something I saw last night on the subway back to Brooklyn."

"I live in Brooklyn too," Daniel said. "North Gowanus."

"I live in Williamsburg," Julie said. "But the men I saw were going to North Gowanus. I think they were ironworkers, and they were being mean to a boy your age. They called him 'lazy punk'."

"They weren't being mean—they were just toughening him up," Daniel said. "When the men were young, they were treated the same way."

"I think I understand," Julie said. "But if someone told me not to make a mistake, I'd be so nervous I'd probably make ten!"

Daniel laughed. "I think you'd be better off working on the ground."

"Are there jobs that aren't dangerous?" Julie asked.

"They're all dangerous," Daniel said, "but some are less risky than others. Some ironworkers install metal stairways and windows. Others put together steel, cast iron, and aluminum. The list goes on."

"I've been collecting newspaper articles about the Empire State Building for almost a year," Julie said, "but I've never read about any of this."

"Maybe people aren't interested," Daniel said.

"Well I am," Julie said. "Out of all the jobs you've described, I think being a riveter sounds the best."

"They only make $1.92 an hour," Daniel said.

"But hoisting engineers make $2.31 an hour."

"I guess I'm in the wrong business!" Julie said, looking down at her piecework. "I only make fifteen cents per piece!"

"At least you like what you do," Daniel said.

"I like it for now," Julie said, "but one day I'm going to be an architect. Maybe I'll design a building that you can build. But I don't think you should work on it unless you really like the job."

"I'll do it whether I like it or not," Daniel said. "It's more than a family tradition. It's the only way I can prove my manhood."

"My father's a brave, strong man, and he doesn't walk in the sky," Julie said. "He sits in an office and draws plans for buildings—at least he did." She remembered her father sitting on a park bench.

"Why doesn't he any more?" Daniel asked, noticing Julie's sudden change of mood.

"He doesn't have any business," Julie said. "At least I don't think he does. I saw him in the park during work hours. He doesn't know I saw him. Now I don't know what to do. I mean, I'm making some money but not enough to support my family. No one in my family even knows I'm working . . ."

"I'm sure it will be all right," Daniel said.

Though it felt strange to be blurting out her secrets to a strange boy, Julie felt a sense of relief. Once she started talking, it was hard to stop.

"I'm thinking about telling my father I saw him," Julie said. "I want him to know that I understand and I love him anyway."

"I wouldn't confront him if I were you," Daniel advised. "It sounds like your father has a lot of pride. He probably wants to deal with his problem alone. That's what men do. He'll talk when he's ready."

"Do you really think he will?" Julie asked.

Daniel shrugged. "Probably. Why don't you tell him that you're working in Manhattan?"

"Because I don't want him to worry," Julie said.

"And he doesn't want you to worry," Daniel said. "You should know how that feels."

Julie was grateful for a boy's point of view.

"I felt a raindrop," Daniel said, looking up.

"Me too," Julie said, putting the embroidery into her bag and standing. "Come on."

As the rain turned into a downpour, they raced to the library past the two stone lions, up the steps, and through the library doors. The entrance hall was crowded and slippery.

"I shouldn't be wearing my work clothes in here," Daniel said, uncomfortably.

"It's all right," Julie said. "It's so crowded, no one will notice." She led Daniel into the high-ceilinged main reference room where they both looked around with awe at the stained glass windows, the detailed, dark wood ceiling, and the shiny wood tables. Marble shelves surrounded the room.

"Do you read much?" Daniel asked.

"All the time," Julie said. "How about you?"

"I don't have much time to read," Daniel said, "but my nine-year-old sister reads all the time. I think you'd like her. She sews too." He noticed an

empty chair and pulled it out for Julie.

"Thank you," Julie said. Just then, a man next to her stood up and Daniel sat down.

"So how often do you go back to the reservation?" Julie asked.

"One weekend a month," Daniel said. "The Caughnawaga Reservation is twelve hours away in Quebec, Canada."

"That's a whole other country!" Julie exclaimed, pulling out her embroidery. "By the time you get there, it's probably almost time to come back!" She began to finish up the third collar.

"Shh," a woman hissed from across the table.

"It's worth the trip," Daniel whispered. "We all miss our families while we're on a job, and a job could last over a year. All the women worry about us."

"I would hate to be gone from my family that long." Julie whispered. "How do you get back?"

"We drive," Daniel said. "My father has a black '27 Buick. My brother and I painted symbols for the different Iroquois clans on the back. Mohawks are a part of the Iroquois, the Six Nations."

"I'd like to see it some time," Julie said. Then she felt a little strange. It didn't seem likely that she'd ever see this boy again. But the more he talked the more she liked him. She was fascinated by Daniel's description of life on the Caughnawaga Reservation. Julie tried to imagine living in a place where there were lakes and open fields. She wondered if it was like the Catskills.

When the afternoon sun filtered through the

stained glass windows, Julie realized it must have stopped raining. She tucked the finished embroidery into her bag. "Let's go," she said. "It's getting late." She was reluctant to leave, but she knew Aunt Esther and Uncle Morris would be happy that she had finished a day early.

"I'd better head back to Brooklyn," Daniel said. "I've got to face the men again, otherwise they'll think I'm a lazy punk."

"I'll walk you toward the station," Julie said. "My aunt and uncle's factory is just south of there."

As they walked west, Julie suddenly felt shy. Though she and Daniel had talked for nearly three hours, she was now aware that she—eleven-year-old Julie Mae Singer—was walking through Manhattan with a handsome boy! Her family would be shocked if they knew. "Is he Jewish?" would be her mother's first question. But no, Daniel was a Mohawk Indian who was helping to build the Empire State Building! She wondered what Sophie and Sam would think of him.

"Good-bye, Julie," Daniel said when they reached Penn Station. "I had a nice time." He caught her eyes.

"Me too," Julie said, blushing. He had such beautiful brown eyes. "I—"

"Maybe we could . . . ," Daniel looked away, suddenly seeming uncomfortable. "I'd better go." He gave Julie a little wave and then hurried toward the station.

"Good-bye, Daniel," Julie called, as she watched him disappear through the glass doors. She wondered if she'd ever see him again.

NINE

WHEN JULIE REACHED THE FACTORY, she was surprised to find the back office door closed.

"They're busy in there," Lucy said, from her place at the long table.

"Should I knock?" Julie asked. "I have something for them, and I have to catch a train back to Brooklyn."

"I'll give it to them," Lucy said, getting up.

"I'll wait a few minutes," Julie said, sitting on a stool outside the office door.

"Suit yourself," Lucy said, picking up her work.

If Nettie had offered, Julie would have given her the piecework. But she didn't trust Lucy.

"Where's Nettie?" Julie asked, looking around.

"She no longer works here," Lucy said, brushing a damp wisp of hair out of her eyes.

"What?" Julie asked with surprise. "Did my aunt and uncle . . . did they have to let her go?"

"No," Lucy said. "Nettie's husband lost his job at the plaster mill, so they're moving to Detroit. He thinks he can get a job there."

"Did Nettie want to go?" Julie asked.

"That didn't matter," Lucy said. "There's no way she could have supported their six children on what she's earning here."

"That's too bad," Julie said. "I like Nettie."

"We all do," Lucy said. "Especially the bosses."

Suddenly the office door opened. "Julie," Aunt Esther said. She looked tired and upset. "I didn't expect you today. Let's see what you brought."

Julie followed her aunt into the office. Uncle Morris was sitting with his head in his hands. "Is everything okay?" Julie asked.

"Nettie left," Aunt Esther said from the doorway.

"I'm sorry to hear that," Julie said.

"So are we," Uncle Morris said. "We always depended on her to do the intricate jobs. The other seamstresses aren't nearly as good as she was—or as quick."

"Let's see what you brought," Aunt Esther said, clearing a space on her desk. Julie pulled the three collars out of her bag and lay them on the desk.

"Lovely!" Aunt Esther exclaimed, after she'd had a chance to inspect them closely. "How would you feel about doing more?"

"You know I want work," Julie said, beaming.

"Good," said Uncle Morris, "because we'd like you to do what Nettie wasn't able to finish. Your aunt and I were talking about this before you came."

"I'll do it," said Julie, "but am I good enough?"

"Definitely," Uncle Morris said, reaching into a basket of half finished dress collars beside his desk and handing one to Julie. "See, it's no more difficult than that shawl you made for Grandma."

Julie examined the embroidery. It did look simple. "But, will I be taking work away from Lucy or anyone else?"

"Don't worry about that, dear," Aunt Esther said. "There's enough work to go around." She set the basket of collars on her desk. "I'd like to give you six collars today if you think you can finish them by Friday. That'll give you two days."

"I'll take seven," Julie said, unable to believe her good luck. "But I really should be going."

"Before I forget," Uncle Morris said, reaching into his pocket. "Here." He handed Julie forty-five cents. "Thanks for a job well done."

"Thanks for the work," Julie said, smiling. For the first time, she had earned her own money.

*   *   *

Julie arrived at Pennsylvania Station half an hour later than she'd gotten there the evening before. Luckily, the train came right away. When it arrived at the elevated stop in Williamsburg, Julie hurried off the train and raced home through puddles and mud. When she reached Ross Street, she was relieved to see Sam and Sophie playing kick-the-can with their friends. She slowed down to catch her breath.

"Hi, Julie," Rachel Rabinowitz called from her stoop. "Why were you running?" Mikey Peterson sat next to her looking miserable.

"No reason, Rachel," Julie said. "Hi, Mikey."

"Hi," Mikey muttered, staring down at his shoes.

"What's wrong with you?" Julie asked, hoping it was nothing she had done.

"I set Mikey straight," Rachel said. "I told him

that you only like him as a friend. Nothing more."

"That's my business, Rachel," Julie said with annoyance. She turned to Mikey. "I like you as a friend, but a *good* friend, Mikey. I'm just not interested in having a boyfriend right now."

"Don't you think you should give the bracelet back?" Rachel said. "I'm sure Mikey would rather give it to a girl who really wants it." She fluttered her eyelashes.

Julie handed the bracelet to Mikey. "I guess I shouldn't have worn it in the first place."

"Thanks," Mikey said, unable to meet her eye.

"It'll fit me perfectly," Rachel said, reaching out to Mikey.

"I think I'm going to wear it for now," Mikey said. "It's not just for girls." Rachel looked disappointed.

"Your mama was looking for you," Rachel said, stealing a quick glance at Julie.

"When?" asked Julie, gazing across the street.

"A little while ago," Rachel said.

"Julie! Mama wants you to go inside!" Sophie called from down the block.

"Where were you?" Mrs. Singer cried as soon as she saw her youngest daughter. Julie could tell she had been upset for a while.

"I was at the Y—"

"Don't make up stories, Julie," her mother said. "You were in Manhattan."

Julie felt queasy. How did her mother find out?

"Mrs. Kimmelman saw you coming out of the New York Public Library," Mrs. Singer continued.

"Not the Brooklyn Public Library—the New York Public Library! What in the world were you doing there today, and who was the boy you were with?"

Julie's heart raced. It was hard to think fast while she was nervous. She couldn't be completely honest even if she wanted to, now that her aunt and uncle were involved. Suddenly she had an idea.

"I'm sorry, Mama," she said. "I wanted to see how the Empire State Building was progressing. You know how much I've—"

"You went to Manhattan by yourself?" Mrs. Singer cried. "And the strange boy?"

"It started raining," Julie said, speaking slowly so she'd have more time to think. "So I went inside to stay dry. A boy inside needed help finding a book. Should I not have helped him?"

"I'm just glad you're all right," Mrs. Singer said, ignoring the question. "I was so worried about you. Even Sophie wouldn't go into the city by herself."

"You went into Manhattan by yourself, Julie?"

Julie turned to find Sophie in the doorway.

"Who was the strange boy?" she asked.

Julie repeated what she had told her mother. "That's all I know about him."

"I can't believe it," Sophie said. "Wait till Sam hears this." She ran downstairs again.

"Is this the first time you've done this?" Mrs. Singer asked.

Julie nodded, wishing her mother would stop asking questions. She dreaded having her father find out at dinner.

*　　*　　*

Sam was impressed with his younger sister's adventure, and Mr. Singer wasn't nearly as upset as his wife had been. "Just don't do it again, Julie," he said, sounding distracted. "Keeping secrets like that is very wrong." He suddenly looked uncomfortable.

But you do it, Julie wanted to shout.

That night, Julie was reading in her room when Sophie came in to get ready for bed. "I'm really impressed, Julie. I never thought you were capable of going to Manhattan on your own."

"It wasn't that big a deal," Julie said. "I just took the train to Penn Station."

"And then what?" Sophie asked. "Tell me everything." Julie sighed. Sophie had never been known to keep a secret. "I'll tell you a secret if you tell me yours," Sophie said. "I have a crush on Tony Speroni. There. Now tell me yours."

"I already knew that," Julie said. Sophie looked disappointed. "Well, if you promise not to tell . . ." Julie said, making room for Sophie on her bed.

"I know I'm not good at keeping secrets," Sophie said, "but this time I will. I promise."

Without another thought, Julie told Sophie everything, beginning with seeing their father in the park. She told her about going to the factory, getting piecework, seeing the Empire State Building, working in Bryant Park, and meeting Daniel A. Hill.

"I can't believe it, Julie," Sophie said. "Especially the part about Papa. He must feel so awful. Do you think we'll run out of money?"

"I don't know," Julie said. "Every time I pass a breadline I wonder if we'll be standing in one soon."

"I know what you mean," said Sophie, shivering. "How much have you earned?"

"Forty-five cents," Julie said, "but I've only worked a day. Next time it'll be double."

"I'm impressed!" Sophie said. "Maybe Aunt Esther will give me piecework too."

"Don't ask her," Julie said. "I wasn't supposed to tell you. And don't tell Sam. Anyway, you have enough schoolwork to do."

"I guess you have a point," Sophie said, grimacing. "But let's say we did need your money. Where would you say it came from?"

Julie shrugged. "I haven't thought that far ahead. I hope Papa will tell us his secret soon."

"Is there anything I can do?" Sophie asked. She stood up and stretched.

"Cover for me," Julie said. "It didn't help when you said Mikey had been looking for me at lunchtime."

"Sorry about that," Sophie said, looking guilty.

"It's okay," Julie said. "But will you promise not to tell if I do piecework in our room some evenings?"

"My lips are sealed," Sophie said. "Are you going back to Manhattan tomorrow?"

"I don't know," Julie said. "Mama was pretty mad. Maybe I can find a place in Brooklyn. But I'm going to have to go back there eventually."

"Will you see Daniel again?" Sophie asked.

"Probably not," Julie said, but she hoped otherwise.

*   *   *

The next morning Julie found herself heading back to the elevated station. She knew she could probably find a place to do her piecework in Brooklyn if she looked hard enough, but that seemed dull. There were no Skywalkers in Brooklyn. There was no Daniel A. Hill.

When she arrived at Penn Station, she followed the crowds to the site of the Empire State Building. As she peered through a hole in the boarded fence, she realized how much she'd been hoping to see Daniel. Occasionally she saw a boy about his age darting from one place to another, but it was never him. *Maybe he's inside*, she thought. She told herself she'd stay for ten minutes, but when ten minutes were up, she changed it to twenty. Before she knew it, she had been there for an hour and a half! Disappointed, she finally made herself leave. She had work to do.

Julie spent that day and the next two weeks—aside from weekends—doing her piecework in Bryant Park. Everyday she hoped Daniel would show up, and everyday she was disappointed. The more work her aunt and uncle gave her, the less time she had to gaze up at the quickly growing sky-scraper. Usually she watched the Skywalkers while she ate her lunch. She always brought a second sandwich to give to someone less fortunate in the street. At night, she finished her work in her room.

The less time she had to spend on her scrapbook, the more time her father seemed to have for cutting out articles. Every evening she came home to several clippings. Julie knew her father was still out of work. He had determined that the woman who cleaned their house twice a week was a luxury. So, he let her go. Without the extra help, Julie's mother was so busy making meals, shopping, doing laundry, and cleaning the house, she didn't have time to worry about Julie, Sophie, or Sam.

One Friday morning, Julie was surprised to find a larger crowd than usual rushing toward the construction site. She squeezed her way through the crowds, hearing bits and pieces of horrible gossip.

"There was an accident."

"One of the ironworkers fell six flights."

"It must have been a slippery beam."

"Who fell?" Julie asked. "What was his name?" No one seemed to know.

The more Julie heard, the faster she pushed through the crowd, her heart thudding. *Please don't let it be Daniel. Please don't let it be Daniel*, she repeated over and over in her head. She remembered how little confidence he had seemed to have. Had he been forced to conquer his fear and failed?

When she reached the boarded fence, she pushed her way through the crowd to look through a hole. Hundreds of laborers were leaving the site. A sign read: CLOSED FOR THE DAY. A man next to her pointed out Alfred Smith, the president of the Empire State Building, standing toward the front entrance of the building. "He's talking to James Walker, the mayor," the man said. But all Julie could see were

crowds of people. On any other day, Julie would have been excited for the opportunity to see such important New York figures, but today all she cared about was finding Daniel and making sure he was all right.

Remembering the special ambulance entrance on Thirty-third street, she raced back through the crowds. She arrived just in time to see two men carefully sliding a blood-stained stretcher into an ambulance. The sirens were already emitting a high-pitched screech.

Julie caught a glimpse of a dark-haired man wearing a pained expression, climbing into the ambulance. A dark-haired boy climbed in after him—Daniel! Julie sighed with relief knowing he was safe. *But if Daniel is safe*, she thought, *why is he getting into the ambulance?* It had to be a relative— his brother! Had he died? Julie pushed her way toward the ambulance, not knowing what she would do when she reached it.

"Stand back!" ordered a police officer, motioning to Julie and the rest of the crowd.

"Who fell?" Julie asked.

"A young guy named Douglas," the police officer said. "I think he was a structural ironworker. Now get out of the way."

Daniel's brother, Julie realized, horrified. Just as the ambulance turned east, Daniel looked out the window and, for a split second, his sad brown eyes locked with Julie's blue ones.

TEN

JULIE DIDN'T KNOW WHAT TO DO. GOING to Bryant Park was out of the question. She'd never be able to concentrate on her piecework. It was too early to go home and too late to go to the Y.

All she wanted was to see Daniel and tell him everything would be all right—just like she wanted to tell her father. But how could she possibly know? There was no way she could predict that her father would find work or that Douglas would be okay. For all she knew, Douglas could be dead. She shuddered at the thought.

Feeling the need to move, she started walking toward Fifth Avenue, then headed downtown. She was so distracted that she barely noticed the city around her—the high steeple of the Marble Collegiate Church, the delicious smells wafting from the restaurant Delmonico's, the laughter of children in Madison Square Park, the noise of taxicabs, buses, and trolleys coming from the busy intersection where Broadway crossed Fifth Avenue.

"Get out of the way!"

Julie jumped back as a taxicab sped past. She had been so distracted she hadn't stopped before crossing Twenty-third Street. *I must be more careful,* she thought to herself. As she waited to cross, she glanced up at the tall, triangular Flatiron Building that she'd always admired. Today she saw right through it.

When the traffic let up, she crossed the street and continued downtown on Broadway. A poor, old, barefoot man on the sidewalk asked Julie for a nickel. Distracted, she reached into her purse and handed him a coin without even checking to see what it was.

By the time Julie reached Union Square, her feet were beginning to hurt. But she kept on going until she reached Canal Street, where the sidewalks were dense with bargain shoppers. She entered the subway station and boarded a Brooklyn-bound train. Though there were two vacant seats, she stood. It didn't dawn on her until the train was halfway across the Manhattan Bridge that she was not headed toward Williamsburg.

"North Gowanus!" the conductor called as the train came to a stop. Julie realized a small part of her had known where she was going all along.

She left the train feeling both scared and excited. A putrid stench hung in the air. The Gowanus Canal, which ran near the elevated tracks, was the most polluted waterway in the city. *How can anyone live with this smell?* Julie wondered. Was Daniel used to it?

She noticed that she was very high off the ground. At the bottom of the steep stairway, a sign informed her that the North Gowanus station was the highest in the city.

North Gowanus seemed older and shabbier than Williamsburg. Trying not to breathe too deeply, Julie wandered past coal, brick, lumber, and stone yards. Many of the storefronts had VACANT or FOR RENT signs in the windows. *How can I find out where Daniel is staying?* she wondered.

The streets were just as crowded as those in Williamsburg. Laundry men, newsboys, plumbers, salesmen, and junk dealers scurried about doing business. After walking for almost half an hour, Julie decided to ask someone. "Excuse me, sir," she said politely to a man shining another man's shoes. "Do you know where Mr. Hill lives? He's one of the ironworkers at the Empire State Building."

"Sorry, missy," the man said, shrugging.

Next, she asked a mailman.

"I don't know names," the mailman said. "I just know places of residence. And I have no idea if this Mr. Hill is on my route." He suggested she try the bill collector two storefronts down.

"Try Nevins Street," the bill collector said, pointing her in the right direction. "He's probably staying in one of the rooming houses. Those men are good tenants. Always pay their bills on time so I don't have to go after them."

"Thank you, sir," Julie said. As she walked down Nevins Street, she noticed the rooming houses on each side of the street. They all looked similar. Cars were parked along the curb, and trees lined the street. She walked up one side of the street and down the other, unsure of what she was looking for.

She saw another street lined with rooming houses and tried that as well—and then another one.

After an hour, Julie was so exhausted she decided to give up. She turned back the way she came. She wasn't looking forward to going all the way back to Canal Street to switch trains. But if she took a trolley it would take too long.

Something on the back of a black car caught her eye. She went closer and saw six white symbols painted on the trunk—a deer, a beaver, a snipe, a wolf, a bear, and a turtle. *These must be the Iroquois symbols Daniel told me about!* she realized. He and his brother had painted them on their father's Buick—and that was the make of this car!

Julie looked back at the street, hoping for a clue as to which rooming house Daniel, his father, and brother were living in. *They're probably at the hospital*, she told herself. *Or the morgue.* She shivered.

Julie stood near the car to wait. They had to come back at some point. But then she remembered Daniel's advice about her father: "I wouldn't confront him if I were you. He probably wants to deal with his problem by himself."

Maybe Daniel wants to be alone, she thought. *Or with his father and family friends.* Though she thought of him as a friend, they had really only spent a few hours together one afternoon a few weeks earlier. Maybe Daniel had already forgotten about her.

Before walking away, she reached into her purse, pulled out paper and a pencil, and began to write:

Daniel,

*I'm terribly, horribly sorry about
what happened to your brother.
I hope you and your father are all right.
You can always count on me as a friend.
Our conversation meant a lot to me and,
even if we never see each other again,
I'll always remember it.*

*Your friend,
Julie*

She folded the note, stuck it through the partially open car window, and raced back to the elevated station.

*   *   *

When Julie arrived home, Sabbath dinner had already started. "Sorry I'm late," she apologized. She hugged Grandma and then took her seat next to Uncle Morris.

"Don't worry, Julie," Sophie said. "I told Mama and Papa that you often stop at the library on your way home. Remember you told me that?"

Julie nodded, thankful that Sophie had covered for her. Uncle Morris had a sudden coughing attack.

"I didn't think it was open this late," Mr. Singer said, looking with concern at Uncle Morris.

"Sophie meant Mr. Miller's book shop," Julie lied. "I wonder how long he'll stay in business?"

"Did you hear about the accident?" Sam asked Julie as she sat down. "An ironworker fell six stories!"

"*Oy es iz shreklich,*" Grandma said.

"His poor mother," Mrs. Singer said.

"How would I have heard about it?" Julie asked. It felt strange to hear her family talking about her secret in this way. For a second, she wondered if she'd been found out.

"Everyone knows," Sam said. "It was in the evening paper."

"I think I did hear about it," Julie said. She didn't want to lie more than was necessary. She wished her voice didn't sound so shaky. "I didn't know how serious it was though. Did the boy . . . did he . . . " She wasn't sure if she wanted to know.

"He didn't die," Sam said. "But he's in serious condition. Those men are crazy to work so high up."

"You could look at it that way," Mrs. Singer said, "or you could look at them as brave and strong."

Julie looked at her mother with surprise. That was just what she had been thinking.

But the thought of the accident gave Julie a sick feeling in her stomach. Before dessert, she excused herself with a headache, and went to her room. As she lay on her bed, she imagined a telephone ringing on the reservation. *Daniel's poor mother*, she thought, drifting into a fitful sleep.

"Julie," Sophie said, shaking her sister awake. "What's wrong?"

Julie opened her eyes, which felt swollen. "What time is it?" she asked.

"Nine-thirty," Sophie said, sitting on Julie's bed. "I didn't mean to wake you, but you were crying in your sleep. Was it a bad dream?"

Julie shook her head and felt a damp spot on her pillow.

"Then what's wrong?" Sophie asked. "You can tell me."

"The boy who fell was Daniel's brother, Douglas," Julie said.

Sophie thought for a few seconds. "The boy you met at Bryant Park?" she asked.

Julie nodded, her eyes filling with tears again.

"I'm so sorry," Sophie said, embracing her sister. "Maybe he'll be okay."

Julie hoped so.

*   *   *

It rained the entire weekend, so no one thought it odd that Julie spent most of the time in her room. "She's working on her scrapbook," Sophie told Mr. and Mrs. Singer. But Julie was really embroidering dress collars. The piecework was such a good distraction that she finished all of it.

By Monday morning, Julie had realized that there was nothing she could do about Daniel's situation. When she arrived in Manhattan, she planned to go straight to her aunt and uncle's factory. But her eyes automatically wandered up to the Empire State Building. Unable to resist, she walked east toward the construction site. She was surprised to see the

Skywalkers back at work so soon after the accident. It seemed disrespectful. *Couldn't they have waited a week or so?* she thought. As she watched them balancing on narrow beams, she wondered if they were more fearful than usual. How could they not be thinking about Douglas?

As she neared Fifth Avenue, the crowd became unbearable. It seemed to be growing along with the number of people who had lost their jobs. *Daniel won't be there*, she told herself. She turned and hurried over to the factory.

When Julie arrived, the door to her aunt and uncle's office was closed.

"I wouldn't go in there if I were you," Lucy said. "Leave your piecework with me."

"I'll wait," Julie said. Just as she sat on the stool, the door swung open. Suddenly, she found herself face to face with her father!

ELEVEN

"JULIE!" MR. SINGER EXCLAIMED. "WHAT in the world are you doing here?"

"I . . . uh . . ." Julie began. She looked helplessly at Aunt Esther and Uncle Morris.

"Be honest with your father," Aunt Esther said, brushing a piece of lint off her dress. "He's been very honest with us."

"Honest?" Julie asked, looking at her father.

"I have some things to tell you, Sophie, and Sam," he said. "I've already spoken to your mother. But first I want to know what you're doing here."

"It's a long story, Papa," Julie said, not knowing where to start. She felt partly nervous and partly relieved to have the chance to tell the truth.

"I have as much time as you need," Mr. Singer said.

"I saw you in Fort Greene Park when you were supposed to be working, Papa," Julie began.

"We didn't know about that," Uncle Morris said.

"What exactly do you know, Morris?" Mr. Singer asked.

"Don't get mad at Uncle Morris or Aunt Esther," Julie said. "This whole thing is my fault. When I realized you had no work, I got scared, so I begged Aunt Esther to give me a job."

"A job?" Mr. Singer looked surprised.

"I'm sorry, David," Aunt Esther said, coming to Julie's rescue. "Julie came to me and asked for job at the factory. I said no, but she wanted it so desperately. You know how stubborn your younger daughter can be. I gave her some piecework—I knew she could handle it. I really didn't plan on giving her as much as I've been giving her, but Nettie left and we haven't been able to replace her yet. I had no idea she knew you were out of work. We didn't know till today."

"You told them?" Julie stared at her father. He seemed to be in better spirits than usual.

Mr. Singer nodded. "I feel much better having everything in the open. I'm so ashamed of the way I've acted lately, but I didn't want anyone to worry. Every architect I know is having a hard time finding work and collecting money. My two biggest clients can't pay their bills, and the man I've been designing the Park Avenue townhouse for cancelled the job. Few people have money to spend on anything other than food for their families—if they're lucky enough to have that."

"I'm really sorry, Papa," Julie said.

"In most cases, I would punish you—especially for coming into the city by yourself," Mr. Singer said. "Your mother and I have told you before that you are never to come to Manhattan alone. Do you realize how dangerous that was?"

Julie nodded, although she hadn't felt scared at all.

"But how can I get mad at you for keeping a secret when I was doing the same thing myself?" Mr. Singer added.

"Good point," said Uncle Morris. "Now let's see what Julie has brought us." Julie spread the nine embroidered dress collars on his desk.

"Lovely," Aunt Esther said, admiring the perfect stitches.

"Your daughter has talent," Uncle Morris said.

"She sure does," Mr. Singer said, proudly. "Now, we need to go. I have to talk to Sophie and Sam."

"Wait," Uncle Morris said. He reached into a drawer and handed Julie a dollar and thirty-five cents.

"That's more money than I've earned all week," Mr. Singer said wryly.

"Why don't you take it, Papa," Julie said, suddenly feeling uncomfortable. She offered him the cash.

"Don't be silly," Mr. Singer said, with a twinkle in his eye. "We'll be fine. I withdrew all of our savings from the bank before it went out of business. We just have to be frugal since I'm not earning anything. Your aunt and uncle are going to help us out until I can find work."

"We're happy to help," Aunt Esther said, ruffling Julie's hair.

"Soon unemployed architects will be able to register for any work available," Mr. Singer said. "It's a program sponsored by a committee that represents almost every New York architectural firm. I'm not sure how much it will help, but at least it's something."

"Can I still do piecework?" Julie asked hopefully.

"We'll talk to your mother about it," Mr. Singer said. "She's not going to be happy when she hears what's been going on—especially since you've gone against your word. If we decide to let you continue, I know she'll want you to work at home rather than . . ."

"Where *have* you been working?" Uncle Morris raised an eyebrow.

"In Bryant Park," Julie said.

"David, if I had known she was sewing in a city park among strangers I'd have never let—"

"What's done is done, Esther," Mr. Singer said. "I'm just thankful she's here in one piece. Let's go, Julie."

As Julie and her father walked toward Penn Station, Julie began to feel nervous about telling her mother the truth.

"What a spectacular sight!" Mr. Singer said, squinting into the sun. "I'll bet those are the Indians living in North Gowanus."

"They are," Julie said. "I met the son of one of the Skywalkers in Bryant Park."

"You met one of the Skywalkers?" Mr. Singer said in amazement. "I always thought Sophie was the one I'd have to worry about when it came to young men."

"You don't have to worry about me. The boy was very nice, and he told me a lot about ironworkers. His brother is the one who fell on Friday," she said, feeling sad again.

*   *   *

Mrs. Singer was just as upset as Julie had expected her to be. She sunk onto the sofa, not knowing whom to

be more upset with—Aunt Esther or Julie. Julie felt grateful to have her father on her side.

"This whole thing is my fault," Mr. Singer said. He sat down on a chair beside the door and patted Julie on the shoulder. "When Julie saw me in the park she got scared."

Julie smiled weakly. "I'm—"

"What's going on?" Sam asked. He and Sophie entered the room.

"Your sister has been sneaking into Manhattan every day for the past three weeks," Mrs. Singer said.

"You told them, Julie?" Sophie asked with surprise. She gave her mother a guilty look. "Julie told me it was a secret."

"Papa was at the factory when I delivered the dress collars today," Julie said.

"You'll be punished, Julie," her mother said, looking at her husband. "Manhattan can be very dangerous for an eleven-year-old girl."

"If you punish Julie, you have to punish me," said Mr. Singer. "I kept just as big a secret as she did."

Sam looked impressed. "What kind of secret have you been keeping, Papa?"

Mr. Singer told them what he had already told everyone else.

"Are we going to have to move?" Sam asked.

"Do we have enough money for food?" Sophie asked.

"You have nothing to worry about now," Mr. Singer said. "But as I've said before, we're going to have to give up things that aren't absolutely necessary."

"Can I keep doing piecework?" Julie asked, looking from her mother to her father.

"Absolutely not," Mrs. Singer said.

"Actually, Hannah, I've thought about it, and I don't think it's a bad idea," Mr. Singer said. "Since Esther and Morris will be helping us out, it would be nice to give them something back. If Julie continues doing piecework, they won't have to hire someone else to take Nettie's place."

"Can Sam and I do piecework?" Sophie asked.

"You won't catch me doing embroidery," Sam said. "But maybe I can help out with deliveries. It would sure beat studying for my bar mitzvah."

"You're going to study for your bar mitzvah no matter what," Mr. Singer said, "but maybe you can do both. I'll talk to your aunt and uncle."

That night, Julie slept better than she had in weeks. She was earning her own money, and there was no longer anything devious about it.

TWELVE

THE FOLLOWING MONDAY MORNING, THE whole family went to Manhattan together. Mrs. Singer and Sophie, now finished with summer school, were doing piecework with Julie, and today was Sam's first day as a delivery boy for Aunt Esther and Uncle Morris.

On the way to the factory, Mr. Singer announced that he had good news. "We're going to spend the weekend in Coney Island," Mr. Singer said.

Julie, Sophie, and Sam cheered.

"You'll have to be on your best behavior," Mr. Singer continued. "We're going to be staying at the home of a client of mine. And you'll have to spend your own money on all extras—but don't go crazy. I'll take care of our meals, of course, and the beach is free." Everyone thought this very fair.

Julie, Sophie, and Mrs. Singer spent the morning doing piecework at the long tables. If Lucy was unhappy about having three new embroiderers, she kept her feelings to herself. She didn't want to lose her job over having bad manners.

Uncle Morris took Sam to make his first delivery, while Mr. Singer designed some storage shelves.

After lunch, they all took a walk to the site of the Empire State Building, their eyes constantly wandering up to the 102-story mooring mast. The closer they got, the more nervous Julie felt. She hadn't been there since Douglas's accident.

"There's your friend, Julie," Sophie teased, pointing toward the top of the tall steel structure.

"It's not him," Julie said. "He wasn't a Skywalker yet. I'm sure he isn't there anyway—not after his brother's accident."

"I want to meet him," Sam said.

"Don't count on it, Sammy," Julie said. "He probably went back home."

Not wanting to fight the crowds, Mrs. Singer and Aunt Esther decided to look in the windows of B. Altman. Mr. Singer and Uncle Morris stood on the outskirts of the crowd looking up.

"I want the three of you to stay together," Mr. Singer said.

"We will," said Sophie as she and Sam followed Julie into the crowd. Julie led them toward the boarded fence. They took turns looking through the hole.

"Let's go back," Sophie said, twenty minutes later. "I have a cramp in my neck."

"I'm ready," Sam said.

"Me too," Julie said, trying to hide her disappointment. As much as she had told herself Daniel wouldn't be there, she couldn't help hoping. With low spirits, she squeezed through the crowd with Sam and Sophie.

Suddenly, Julie felt a tap on her shoulder. She turned and found herself staring into a pair of dark eyes.

"Daniel!" she gasped.

"I got your note, Julie," Daniel said, brushing a dark strand of hair from his face. "I didn't know where to find you. I went back to Bryant Park, but you weren't there."

"I felt so terrible when I heard about Douglas . . ." Julie began.

"I know," Daniel said, looking relaxed and peaceful. "He'll be back at work in a year or so."

"Is he crazy?" Julie asked with horror.

Daniel shrugged. "Maybe he is. But a Skywalker's work is his life."

"Are you still planning to become a Skywalker?" Julie asked, unsure she wanted to hear Daniel's answer.

"Not anymore," Daniel said, smiling. "Remember when you said I don't have to be a Skywalker to prove my manhood?" Julie nodded. "Well, you were right. Our conversation meant a lot to me, Julie."

"I'm glad," Julie said. "After what happened, I'm sure you won't walk on the high steel beams now because—"

"I did it," Daniel interrupted.

"Did what?" Julie asked.

"Last week I walked out on the same beam my brother fell from. It was on the thirty-seventh floor."

Julie's jaw dropped open in amazement.

"Julie!"

"I'll be there in a minute," Julie called to Sophie who stood with Sam, several feet away. She turned back to Daniel. "Did those men who called you 'slowpoke' make you do it?" she asked suspiciously.

"No, I did it on my own," Daniel said proudly. "It made me feel closer to my brother."

"But if you agreed about not having to prove your manhood that way—" Julie shook her head.

"I said I did it," Daniel explained, "for the first and last time. After Douglas fell, my father and I had a long talk. He said it was my choice as to whether or not I wanted to carry on the family tradition of being an ironworker. He said he'd support me if I decided to do something else with my life. It was hard enough for him to see one son get hurt, and he didn't want to see it happen again. So I was honest with him. And this is my last day here. Tomorrow I'm going back to the reservation to learn to be a carpenter."

"How wonderful for you!" Julie said, wondering if she'd ever see him again.

"What about you?" he asked. "Still working?"

"Yes," Julie said, "but now my father knows. You were right when you said he probably wanted to handle his problem alone. He ended up telling us his secret—but only when he was ready. Now my aunt and uncle are helping us out with money, and my mother, brother, and sister are working for them."

"Aren't you going to introduce us?" said Sophie.

Julie turned around to find her brother and sister standing behind her.

"Daniel, this is my sister and brother, Sophie and Sam," Julie said.

"We're sorry your brother got hurt," Sophie said.

"He broke both legs, one arm, and four ribs," Daniel said, "but he's going to be okay."

"Ouch!" Sam said. "That sounds pretty bad."

"We've all seen worse," Daniel said, looking up toward the mooring mast. "I was upset, but your sister was a comfort." Daniel winked at Julie. Sophie looked at her in astonishment.

"Daniel!" called a gruff voice.

Daniel turned and waved to a man who looked like him.

"That's my father," Daniel said. "I've got to go, Julie, but if you give me your address I'll write."

"Really?" Julie asked. She fumbled in her purse and pulled out a pencil and a scrap of paper.

"Yes, but only if you promise to write back," Daniel said, grinning. "I want you to tell me all about your first elevator trip up to the top of the Empire State Building."

"I'll tell you every detail," Julie promised, scribbling her address and handing the paper to Daniel.

"I've never had a pen pal before," Daniel said, sticking the paper in his pocket.

"Me neither," Julie said.

"Oh—I almost forgot." He reached into his pocket and pulled out a beaded bracelet, similar to the one Mikey's father had found but with an even more spectacular pattern. Yellow and green flowers and leaves were raised on a blue background. "I brought this hoping I'd see you."

"I love it!" Julie exclaimed, letting Daniel fasten it on her wrist. "It's beautiful. Thank you, Daniel." Sophie and Sam looked at it with admiration.

"Where's your other bracelet?" Daniel asked.

"I gave it back to the boy who gave it to me," Julie explained. "It's a long story."

"Well—I have to go," Daniel said, gesturing toward his father. "Good luck with everything."

"Good luck to you, too," Julie said, wishing he didn't have to go. She reached out her hand, and Daniel gave it an awkward squeeze. Before she could say another word, he was gone.

"Poor Mikey," Sam grinned.

"He's handsome!" Sophie whispered over Julie's shoulder.

Julie had been so focused on Daniel she had forgotten that Sophie and Sam were standing behind her. "I know," Julie said, unable to stop smiling. She couldn't wait for the mailman to deliver Daniel's first letter.

SELECTED BIBLIOGRAPHY

- Duffy, Peter. "The Mohawks of Brooklyn." *Brooklyn Bridge*, March 1999.
- Farrell, Jacqueline. *The Great Depression.* World History series. San Diego, CA: Lucent Books, 1996.
- Hill, Richard. *Skywalkers: A History of Indian Ironworkers.* Flushing, Ontario: Woodland Indian Cultural Education Centre, 1987.
- Howe, Irving and Kenneth Libo. *How We Lived, A Documentary History of Immigrant Jews in America, 1880–1930.* New York: Richard Marek, 1979.
- Jackson, Kenneth, ed. *The Encyclopedia of New York City.* New Haven: Yale University Press, 1995.
- James, Jr., Theodore. *The Empire State Building.* New York: Harper & Row, 1975.
- Mitchell, Joseph. "The Mohawks in High Steel." *The New Yorker*, September 17, 1949.
- Talese, Gay. *The Bridge.* New York: Harper & Row, 1964.
- Tauranac, John. *The Empire State Building: The Making of a Landmark.* New York: St. Martin's Griffin, 1995.
- *The Brooklyn Daily Eagle Almanac.* New York: The Brooklyn Daily Eagle, 1929.
- Waldinger, Roger. *Through the Eye of the Needle.* New York: New York University Press, 1986.
- Willensky, Elliot. *When Brooklyn Was the World, 1920–1957.* New York: Harmony Books, 1986.
- Willis, Carol, and Donald Friedman, eds. *Building the Empire State.* New York: W. W. Norton & Co., 1998.